For Jane, Ellen, and Doreen
—J. F.

To Jamey and my mini wolf pack: Samurai, Jinx, Hansel, and Gretel
—E. T.

Published by Two Lions, New York

www.apub.com

Amazon, the Amazon logo, and Two Lions are trademarks of Amazon.com, Inc., or its affiliates.

ISBN-13: 9781503902947 (hardcover)
ISBN-10: 1503902943 (hardcover)

The illustrations are rendered in digital media.

Book design by AndWorld Design
Printed in China

First Edition
1 3 5 7 9 10 8 6 4 2

two lions

IT'S NOT HANSEL AND GRETEL

Written by Josh Funk

Illustrated by Edwardian Taylor

Once upon a time, Hansel and Gretel lived with their mama and papa on the outskirts of the woods.

Hansel? Gretel? Where are you?

It was a time of great famine, and there wasn't enough food. Hansel and Gretel's parents hatched an evil plan to get rid of their children.

Gretel, should we be worried?

Nah, our parents love us.

No, children. You *should* be worried.

That afternoon, Papa took the children deep into the forest.

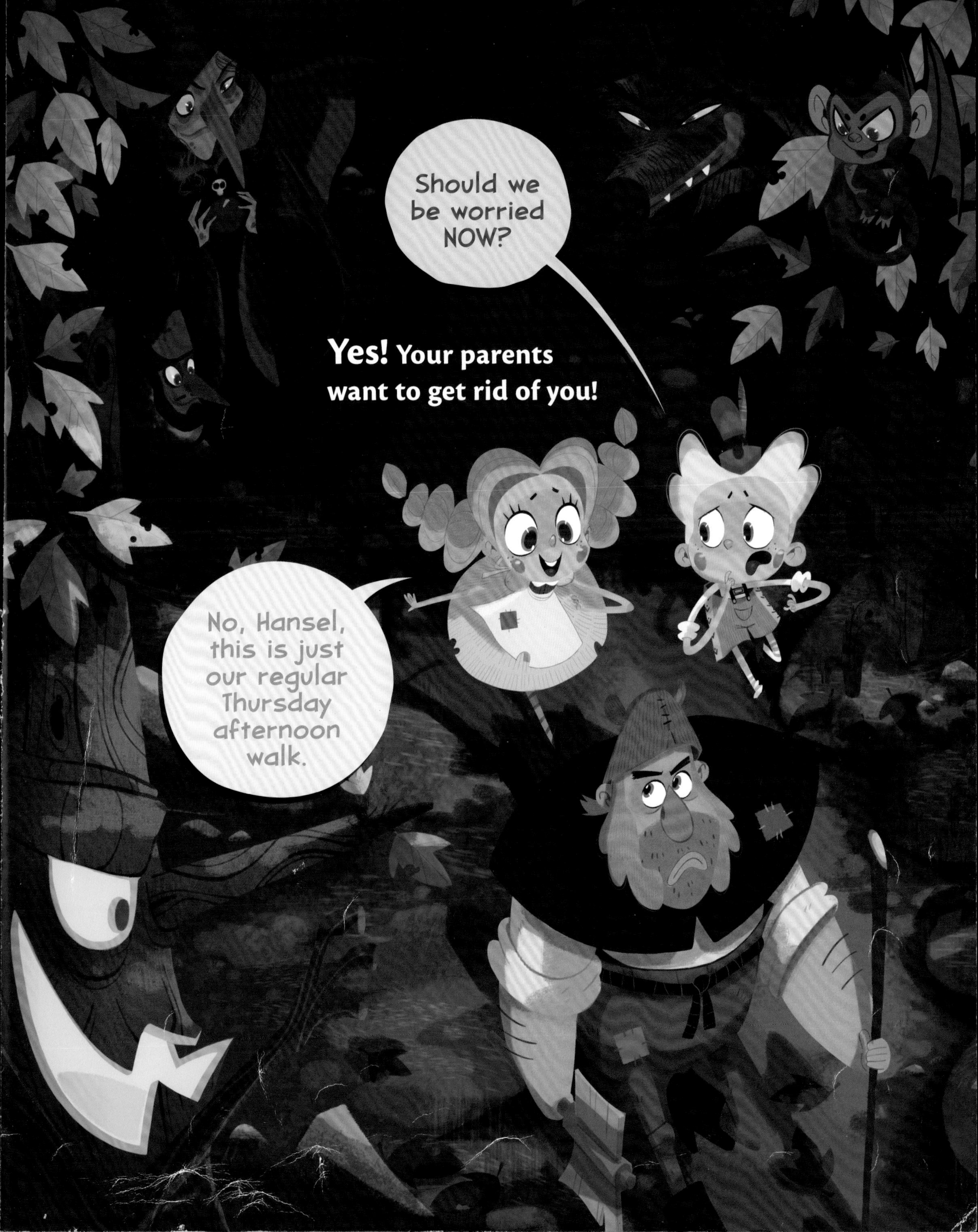

When the sky grew dark, Papa ran off without a word. Hansel and Gretel grew cold and hungry.

Luckily, Hansel had left a trail of bread crumbs leading back home.

The next morning,
Hansel and Gretel were
completely lost. They
began searching for a way
back home but couldn't—

Look!
There's our
house!

What?

YAY!
WE FOUND
IT!

No! You can't find it! That's not how the story goes!
Excuse me, but we've lived on the outskirts of these woods our whole lives. I think we know our way around.
Mama! Papa! We're home!

Gretel, where are Mama and Papa?
Maybe Papa got lost on the way home to get blankets and food. He does have a terrible sense of direction.
NO! HE DIDN'T GET LOST!
But where's Mama? She's not in her workshop.
MOM
She's probably out searching for us.

Hansel and Gretel trekked deeper and deeper into the—

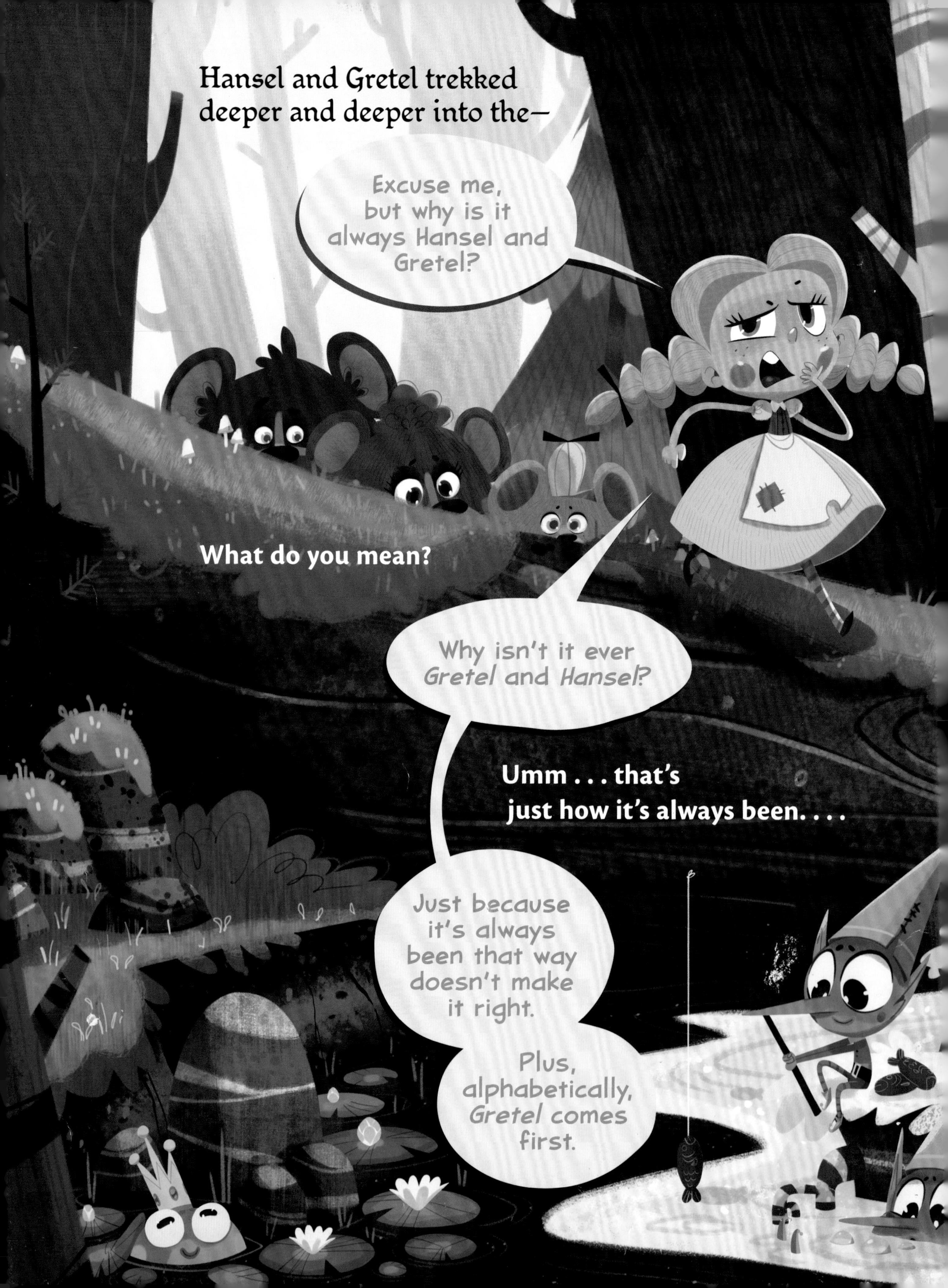

Okay, okay. How's this?
Gretel and Hansel trekked deeper
and deeper into the woods . . .

Much
better.

until they came upon . . .

Come inside from the cold, little dearies. I can put you in my oven to warm you up.
No, you offer them some food!
Oh, but it's so cold! I could use a little oven time.
NO OVEN TIME!

The old lady was really a witch—who liked to eat children!

Don't be silly. She's a sweet old lady.

I promise you, she's a witch!

I don't really have any magical powers, so I'm not exactly a witch.

The witch (who was NOT a sweet old lady) locked Hansel in a cage and forced him to eat candy and treats to fatten him up.

YAY! CANDY!

I wanna be put in the candy cage! Can I go in the candy cage?

No, you can't! Gretel was forced to do chores around the house.

This is ridiculous! The boy gets to sit around and eat candy while the girl has to cook and clean? Get with the times—this is the fifteenth century!

Ugh! Fine!
Hansel **AND** Gretel—

I mean, Gretel **AND** Hansel were locked in a cage and forced to eat candy.

The witch could see that it would be weeks before the children became fat and puffy enough to eat. So—

That is NOT part of the story!
He is NOT allergic to strawberries!
Excuse me, Dr. Storyteller, but food allergies are NOT a joke. They can be VERY serious! Luckily Hansel is only mildly allergic to strawberries!
I'd better start the oven.
NO! It's too soon in the story!

Even though it was far too soon, the witch prepared the oven.
I fink I mokay.
Double, double toil and trouble...
I can't hear you over that noisy oven. Did you say TOILET trouble?
Ugh! I thought you *didn't* want to do chores. Gretel?

"How To GINGERBREAD BOY"

"I don't. But who can say no to such a nice old lady?"

SHE'S A WITCH! I PROMISE!

Hmm, if I borrow some beans from the giant, I can make a little-boy chili.
Oh, are you chilly? Do you need some oven time? Here, I'll help you.
AAHHHHHH!

Gretel, I found this book.
Fifty Recipes for Cooking Children?
You know, something tells me she wasn't such a nice lady after all.
50 Recipes for CHILDREN
YES! That was ME!
I WAS TELLING YOU THAT!
No need to get your undies in a twist!

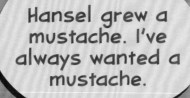

This is ridiculous.

Oh, come on!
A unicorn?!

Next you're gonna tell me that Fluffybottom flew you home to your parents, and you all lived happily ever after.

Unicorns can't fly. Everyone knows that.

Look, Gretel! It's Mama and Papa!

I'm so sorry, children! I got lost on the way home to get blankets and food. You know I have a terrible sense of direction.
What?! No! You had an evil plot!
And I built this flying contraption to go searching for you.
That's exactly what I thought!
This is ALL wrong!

You know, if you take out the "child" ingredient, these recipes aren't half-bad.
Maybe we could live here and open a bakery!
Yes! Let's do it!